P9-APN-330

THE FIRST CHRISTMAS

To Olivia and Grant

—W. M.

SIMON & SCHUSTER BOOKS FOR YOUNG READERS
An imprint of Simon & Schuster Children's Publishing Division
1230 Avenue of the Americas, New York, New York 10020
© 2021 by Will Moses
Book design by Krista Vossen © 2021 by Simon & Schuster, Inc.
All rights reserved, including the right of reproduction in whole or in part in any form.
SIMON & SCHUSTER BOOKS FOR YOUNG READERS is a trademark of Simon & Schuster, Inc.
For information about special discounts for bulk purchases, please contact Simon & Schuster Special Sales at 1-866-506-1949
or business@simonandschuster.com.
The Simon & Schuster Speakers Bureau can bring authors to your live event. For more information or to book an event, contact the
Simon & Schuster Speakers Bureau at 1-866-248-3049 or visit our website at www.simonspeakers.com.
The text for this book was set in Edlund.
The illustrations for this book were rendered in oil paint.
Manufactured in China
0621 SCP
First Edition
2 4 6 8 10 9 7 5 3 1
Library of Congress Cataloging-in-Publication Data
Names: Brooks, Phillips, 1835-1893, author. | Moses, Will, illustrator. | Brooks, Phillips, 1835-1893. O little town of Bethlehem.
Title: The first Christmas / [illustrated by] Will Moses ; lyrics by Phillips Brooks.
Description: First edition. | New York : Simon & Schuster Books for Young Readers, [2021] | "A Paula Wiseman book." | Audience: Ages 4-8. |
Audience: Grades 2-3. | Summary: Presents the story of Jesus's birth, based on the lyrics of the carol "O Little Town of Bethlehem."
Identifiers: LCCN 2021000041 (print) | LCCN 2021000042 (ebook) | ISBN 9781534478787 (hardcover) | ISBN 9781534478794 (ebook)
Subjects: LCSH: Jesus Christ—Nativity—Songs and music. | Carols, English—United States—Texts. | Christmas music—Texts. | CYAC:
Jesus Christ—Nativity--Songs and music. | Carols. | Christmas music.
Classification: LCC PZ8.3.B78966 Fi 2021 (print) | LCC PZ8.3.B78966 (ebook) | DDC 782.28/1723 [E]—dc23
LC record available at https://lccn.loc.gov/2021000041
LC ebook record available at https://lccn.loc.gov/2021000042

Luke 2:14 excerpt from the *King James Bible*

THE FIRST CHRISTMAS

✳ WILL MOSES ✳

O Little Town of Bethlehem lyrics by PHILLIPS BROOKS

A Paula Wiseman Book

Simon & Schuster Books for Young Readers

New York   London   Toronto   Sydney   New Delhi

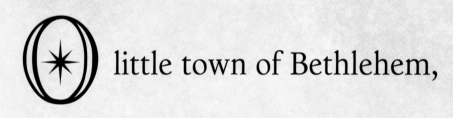little town of Bethlehem,

How still we see thee lie!

Above thy deep and dreamless sleep

The silent stars go by;

Yet in thy dark streets shineth

The everlasting light,

The hopes and fears of all the years

Are met in thee tonight.

For Christ is born of Mary;

And, gathered all above,

While mortals sleep, the angels keep

Their watch of wondering love.

O morning stars together

Proclaim the holy birth;

And praises sing to God the King,

And peace to all on earth.

How silently, how silently,

The wondrous gift is given!

So God imparts to human hearts

The blessing of his heaven.

"Glory to God in the highest, and on earth peace, good will toward men."

—Luke 2:14

O LITTLE TOWN OF BETHLEHEM

Phillips Brooks, 1868

Lewis H. Redner, 1868

How silently, how silently,
The wondrous gift is given!
So God imparts to human hearts
The blessings of his heaven.

No ear may hear his coming,
But in this world of sin,
Where meek souls will receive him still,
The dear Christ enters in

O Holy Child of Bethlehem,
Descend to us, we pray;
Cast out our sin and enter in;
Be born to us today.

We hear the Christmas angels
The great glad tidings tell;
O come to us, abide with us,
Our Lord Emmanuel.

✳ A NOTE ABOUT THE TEXT ✳

Phillips Brooks was the rector of the Church of the Holy Trinity in Philadelphia, Pennsylvania. He wrote the words to "O Little Town of Bethlehem" in 1867. Lewis H. Redner, an organist, put Phillips Brooks's words to music a year later.

Over the generations the song has been, and remains, a favorite of the Christmas season.

AUTHOR'S NOTE

Just about everyone loves Christmastime, but I fear that many of us, and I include myself among the many, sometimes lose sight of the true meaning of Christmas. All too often in today's busy world we have a tendency to think of Christmas as being about gifts, bright decorations, and parties. I am not opposed to any of these activities, but we should also take time from our holiday reveling to remember and celebrate the true, first Christmas story, the birth of Jesus Christ. Please enjoy this story however you come to find it. And I hope this book reminds you to take some time to consider that on a night over 2,000 years ago, in a faraway and harsh land, a miracle occurred. Then I hope you might say a little prayer for us all and give thanks for your family, friends, good fortune, and gift of life you enjoy.

Thank you, and please enjoy the book. Merry Christmas!

—Will Moses